When the Moon Shines Brightly on the House

by Ilona Bodden
with illustrations by Hans Poppel

TO SCOTT
HAPPY BIRTHDAY
TO
LOVE YOU
AMANDA

Dec. 16, 1985

BARRON'S

Barron's Educational Series, Inc.

Woodbury, New York • London • Toronto • Sydney

When the moon shines brightly on the house

the mouse comes climbing out of its hole,

has a peek at all the rooms,

takes a ride on Peter's train,

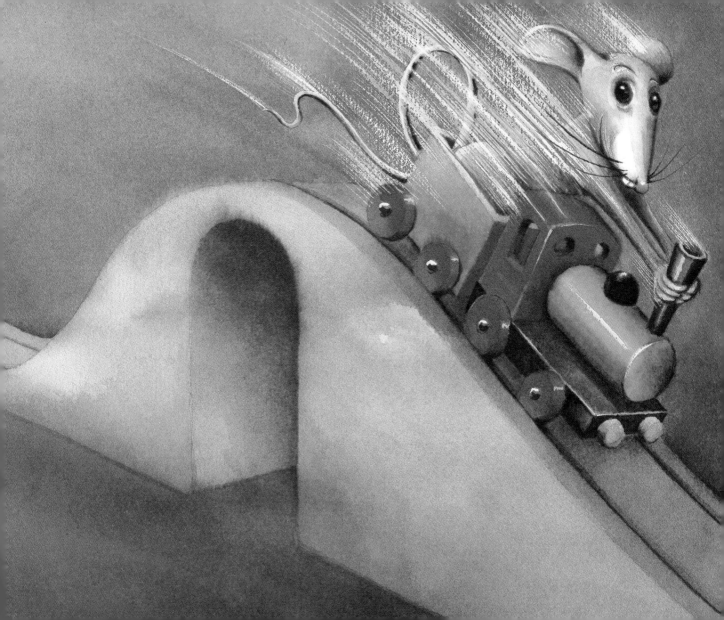

nibbles cheese and tastes the bacon,

flees in panic from the cat,

roams and prowls the whole night long

until the sun smiles in the sky.

Then the mouse creeps back in its hole

to take a rest from its nighttime ramble.